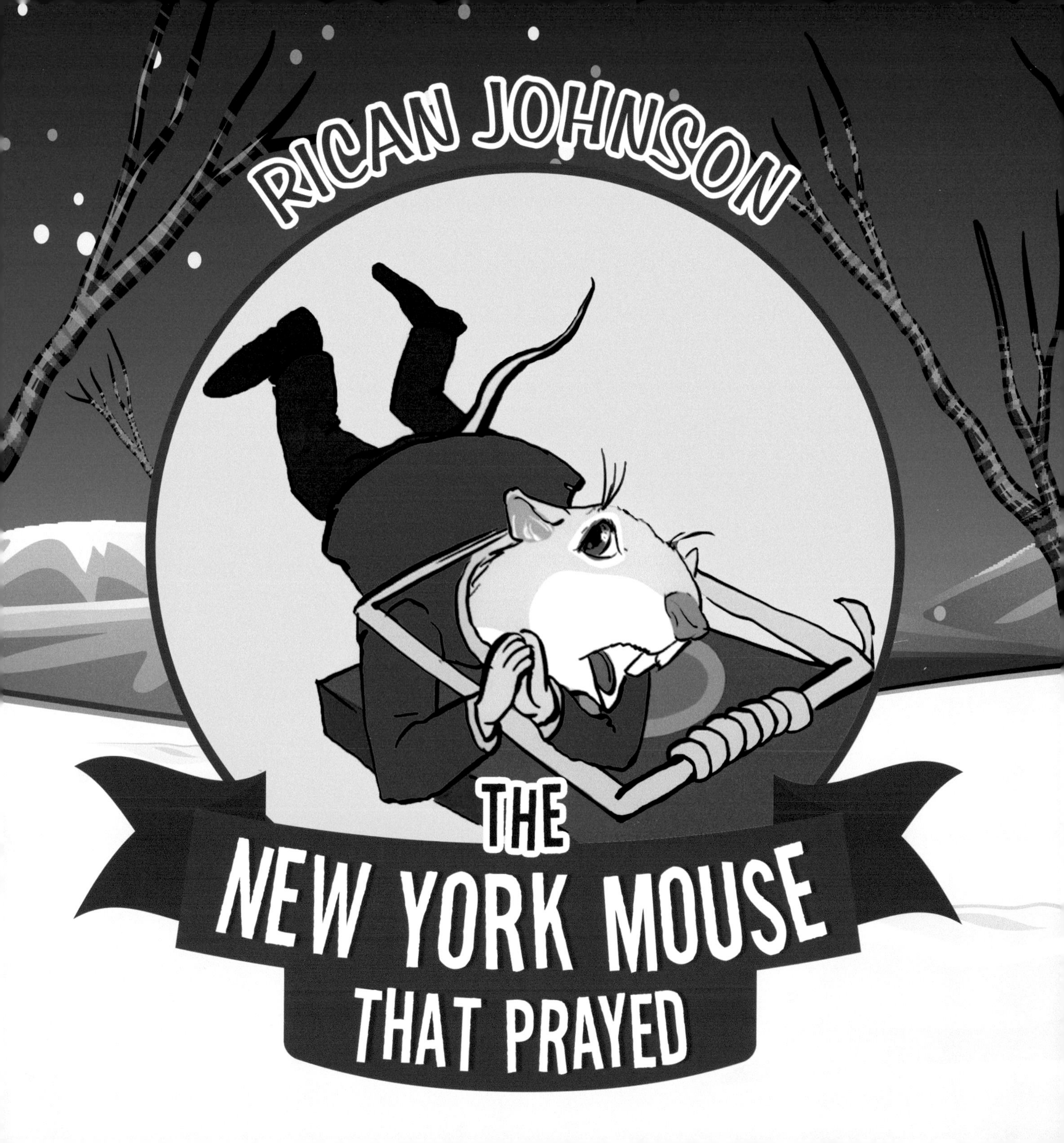
RICAN JOHNSON
THE
NEW YORK MOUSE
THAT PRAYED

To order additional copies of this book, contact:
Xlibris
844-714-8691
www.Xlibris.com
Orders@Xlibris.com

ISBN: 978-1-6698-7901-5 (sc)
ISBN: 978-1-6698-7904-6 (e)

Print information available on the last page

Rev. date: 06/28/2023

THE NEW YORK MOUSE THAT PRAYED

Winter was approaching the beautiful city of New York. A very determined and hardworking mouse by the name of Mr. Jones was very excited by the news, his wife Amiska had told him earlier in the morning before she prepared and gave him his breakfast and sent him off to work. They were expecting to have a new addition to their family because Mrs.Jones is pregnant, and he was so happy! Their son, Alex, would become a big brother, to a baby brother or sister.

"But who knows," said Mr. Jones, "it could be one, two, three or four babies!" "oh yes it could be more, but only God knows" he bursted out laughing! "I can't wait to meet them, "he said."

That day when Mr. Jones arrived at work, he told his boss that he would like to leave work early. He told him about the exciting news that his wife Mrs. Jones, is pregnant and they are expecting to have a new addition to their family. Mr. Sheriff, his boss, Congratulated him and gave him permission to leave work early that day! In Mr. Jones' mind, he was planning on going home to prepare supper for his wife and son, as they would celebrate the good news about their baby or babies that are on the way.

About one block away from his house, Mr. Jones could see a great deal of smoke as he approached his home. As he got nearer, he could see that it was his house that was on fire! Suddenly he began to lose his mind as he thought that his wife and son were in the burning house that was destroyed by the monster-like fire.

Luckily, they had gone to the bakery to get bread, and to the market to get other food items to make dinner, as his wife, Amiska, was planning to prepare a celebration dinner for their family.

"Oh no!!" Mr. Jones wept! twisting and turning while he held his tummy. Suddenly, he then fell to the ground. All he could see was his neighbors and a lot of other strange mice passing by, and no sign of his wife and son. "Oh Lord my tummy!" he cried, Where is my wife and son?"

12

Then walking quickly down the alley was Mrs. Jones and her son Alex. They could see and hear the excitement that was coming from their neighbors and other unfamiliar mice running to and fro, screaming, and shouting while some stood in Awe! with disbelief fixed upon their faces, Mrs. Jones, and her son, Alex stood there in shock as they witnessed a big, thick, black, and monster-like smoke coming from their house. The crowd has now grown bigger and Mr. Jones was to the opposite side of the Alley, so Mrs. Jones could not see or hear him. Approaching from behind was Mrs. Tomwell, the office clerk from Mr. Jones workplace. She touched Mrs. Jones on her shoulder, as they are acquainted with each other and told her that her husband had left work early for home. A thousand things flashed through her mind as she was now thinking that her husband had been burnt to death in the ugly monster like house fire! Mrs. Jones knew how her husband, Mr. Jones, sleeps a lot when he's tired. She suddenly dropped her grocery bags to the ground. Her small, shiny, tiny eyes began to fill with tears, while she held her son, Alex, tightly as they both fell to their knees while she wept! Her poor baby son, Alex, didn't know what was wrong with his mother and why she was crying.

Briskly clearing the crowd, was Mr. Jones who picked up his wife and son from their knees and hugged his wife as if it was the first time that they were seeing each other in years!

With his eyes still filled with tears, he whispered "I love you!" in her ear.

Because the fire had destroyed Mr. and Mrs. Jones' home, Their family was homeless. Their only other option was to ask Mr. Jones' only friend, Conway, to accommodate his family until he rebuilt his home. Mr. Jones knew how selfish his friend was and he knew that he would have made excuses. But despite this, he still swallowed his pride and asked the Conway family for help since his family has now become homeless.

16

Conway his only friend, could not help him since his wife's parents had moved in to live with his family only a week ago, and they would not have enough space in their home for another family.

"It's okay", said Mr. Jones in a sad tone! He bowed his head like a wilted flower in a garden suffering from water loss on a hot summer day, and then he walked away with his family.

Mr. Jones ran out of options so he took his family to stay in the basement of a house that belonged to a human, until he could rebuild his own house.

The skinny human with a clear complexion and big bulging eyes, looked very scary with his hunch back, scared Mrs. Jones by just his appearance. Mrs. Jones was afraid to leave the basement to go anywhere, even to the market! Because of this, Mr. Jones had to quit work for a short time to stay home with his scared family, who were now living in the basement belonging to the scary looking human!. It was the first time they have been that close to a human.

Winter was finally here and it was snowing heavily, Mr. and Mrs. Jones are now living a good life, enjoying their warm and comfortable new home. Then suddenly, they saw Mr. Peacock, the gossiper. running breathlessly and speechless! His big saggy, eyes could tell that something was wrong, without him even having to open his mouth.

He uttered, "It took me so long to find your new home he smiled while showing his chipped teeth. then told the Jones family what had happened to their friend Conway's house. "it was destroyed during the snow storm", said Mr.Peacock. "Hold on for a minute!" said Mr. Jones, "let me grab my coat and winter hat, because it's still snowing outside".

26

Away they went! They left the house in search of Conway and his family. In an old, ragged car, parked on the roadway they found Conway and his family. Conway smiled and hugged his friends and thanked them for coming out into the snowy mountain to search for him and his family.

Mr. Peacock found an opportunity during an emotional moment to burst out in laughter: "this is all you guys have left, only the clothes to your backs?" Suddenly he stopped laughing, "I really don't know how to handle a bad situation" he said, "but with my tailoring skills I will make you guys some new clothes, with just the turning of some threads".

"come on! Let's go now before it starts to snow heavily again." said Mr. Jones. "Come let me take you guys to my new home; it's very big! "it even has heat to keep us warm during the heavy winter snow, that brings cold days and weakened bones," he said, with a smile.

"I guess it's time for me to go home now", said Mr. Peacock. "I'll see you guys", he smiled saying bye. They all said bye to each other, but just before Mr. Peacock could reach any further, Conway shouted "Bye Chipped!" while his wife added, "Teeth!" "Chipped Teeth is the name", said Conway.

They laughed all the way to Mr. Jones' new home.

The next morning, Mr. Jones went inside the kitchen of the scary-looking human to see what he could find to prepare for breakfast for his family and guests. It was snowing very heavily outside, and he could not go to the market. Mr. Jones managed to take a piece of bread, egg, and cheese from the kitchen counter. that the human prepared for his breakfast so he could eat and head out for work.

Myrie's big, bulging eyes seemed as if they were going to pop right out of his head! so scared was he, that he nearly dropped dead. when he saw Mr. Jones the mouse in his kitchen running away with his breakfast! that consisted of cheese, toast and eggs!

Myrie was running late so he left his house angrily screaming: "We shall meet again and it won't be nice, you little scary, hairy looking thing!" He then added, "I shall fix your business, for today shall be your last, you better eat all you can and have a blast!" while he slammed his door shut in disgusted".

That same evening, when Myrie arrived home from work, the sight of what remained of his breakfast was enough to send him back straight through the door, and to the corner store he went to buy a mouse trap! "I'll fix the mouse's business!"he said". Arggg! I want this mouse dead, I can't get the sight of him out of my head!" Myrie cried.

31

Mr. Jones did not know that by going back in, Myrie's kitchen would put him in great danger. This time, he was served a nice freshly prepared steak not knowing it was a trap! Poor Mr. Jones had no one to watch over his back! He thought to himself, who could be that nice to him, and there he went, walked right into the trap! Just before he could remove the steak, he was caught onto the mouse trap that was set by Myrie, the human who hated him for invading his home and taking his food. Poor Mr. Jones, twisted and turned but couldn't remove himself from the trap. He was lying there in shock and as tears fell from his weary, watery eyes, he thought of his family. What will happen to him? Will he ever get back home to his beautiful wife, son, and friends?

He bowed his head and started to pray, asking for his safe return home to his family.

Myrie was so tired from work earlier that day, that when he came in from the corner store he just prepared the mouse trap and fell asleep on his sofa. While he was sleeping, he had a strange dream that he drank a magic potion and ended up turning into a mouse. In Myrie's dream,he was fussing and seemed to be afraid:

"I'm a little mouse. This life is too hard for me! where will I get food ? I am so hungry!" he yawned, scratching his fuzzy, hairy tummy. he said to himself,

"I will just have to go and search for food on my own! No one is willing to help me" he said.

While he was searching for food, he was caught in a trap. Scared and shivering, he thought to himself, "What will happen to me? I pray I don't end up dead!"

A human approached him and touched his soft, fuzzy fur. As the human pulled out a sharp, shiny object from her kitchen drawer. She picked up the mouse from the trap in her small hands. Cutting a piece of cheese, she fed him and set him free.

Suddenly, Myrie was awoken from his strange dream, and remembering what he was going to do to the mouse if he ever caught it in his kitchen again, he smiled!

Myrie went into his kitchen and saw the mouse on the trap.

He laughed saying, "I finally caught you and this will be the last time I will ever see your little spoon face in my kitchen again! Hahahaha!"

Walking down to his basement with that mouse trap in one hand and a sharp pointed object in the other, He removed and set Mr.Jones, the mouse, free into a small custom made house that was in his basement that belonged to his grandson, Frannie. Mr. Jones and his family were finally free and extremely happy!

Myrie immediately went upstairs from his basement to his kitchen to get food for his new pets, which were now his best friends. He fed and clothed them everyday and they all lived happily ever after. Myrie had found himself some new friends and Mr. Jones and his family will never have to leave their new home to find food ever again! And there we have it, Mr. Jones would never have to work or lift any of his fuzzy fingers to work for his entire life. Thanks to God for letting Myrie save his life.

The End!

I hope that this book makes you smile.

PRAYER BY MR. JONES THE MOUSE

"Lord Jesus! You created all things equal and free, help me this day as you always do, so that I can return to my family" with the food that you provide for us to eat, 'set me free Jesus' but before you do help this human to understand that animals need food too. Lord God I leave everything in your Righteous hands as I pray. Amen

WORDS AND MEANING

House - A building for human, especially one that is lived in by a family or small group of people.

Mouse - A small rodent that typically has a pointed snout, relatively large ears and eyes, and a long tail.

Prayer - A solemn request for help or expression of thanks addressed to God or an object of worship.

Fire - The light, heat, and especially the flame produced by burning.

Food - Solid or liquid that is intake into the body for nutrients, energy and growth.

Winter - The coldest season of the year. That comes between autumn and spring.

KIDS PUZZLE

```
M O U S E F W
Y R F I R E I
R R J I F H N
I D E O O V T
E N O U N E E
D D S X M E R
R E Y A R P S
```

FIRE
FOOD
FRIEND
HOUSE
MOUSE
MR-JONES
MYRIE
PRAYER
WINTER

Printed in the United States
by Baker & Taylor Publisher Services